W9-AUZ-614

WEEDED

Kids love reading
Choose Your Own Adventure®!

Watch for these titles coming up in the
Choose Your Own Adventure® series.

Ask your bookseller for books you have missed
or visit us at cyoa.com to learn more.

MYSTERY OF THE MAYA

BY R. A. MONTGOMERY

ILLUSTRATED BY
V. PORNKERD, S. YAWEERA & J. DONPLOYPETCH

CHOOSE YOUR OWN ADVENTURE® CLASSICS
A DIVISION OF

CHOOSECO
WAITSFIELD, VERMONT

Illustrated by: V. Pornkerd, S. Yaweera, & J. Donploypetch
Book design: Stacey Boyd, Big Eyedea Visual Design
Chooseco dragon logos designed by: Suzanne Nugent

For information regarding permission, write to:

CHOOSECO

P.O. Box 46
Waitsfield, Vermont 05673
www.cyoa.com

ISBN 10 1-933390-45-X
ISBN 13 978-1-933390-45-1

Published simultaneously in the United States and Canada

Printed in the United States

0 9 8 7 6 5 4

For Anson and Ramsey

And
For Avery and Lila

And for Shannon

BEWARE and WARNING!

This book is different from other books.

You and YOU ALONE are in charge of what happens in this story.

There are dangers, choices, adventures and consequences. YOU must use all of your numerous talents and much of your enormous intelligence. The wrong decision could end in disaster—even death. But, don't despair. At anytime, YOU can go back and make another choice, alter the path of your story, and change its result.

Your best friend Tom goes missing on assignment in Mexico. You have to help find him. Will it require you to take a potion that sends you back in time to the world of the mysterious Mayan civilization? Or is Tom still here in the present day? Can you trust Manuel? Depending on your choices, YOU may become a great Mayan ruler or a double agent fighting a modern revolution. The wrong choice could turn you into a human sacrifice on a bloody altar.

It is night. You are standing on the flat top of a stone pyramid. Men dressed in long green robes crowd around you. They chant and sing in a language you don't understand.

You look into the misty light for your friend Tom. Suddenly, you see him—struggling for his life. He is strapped to an altar, his arms and legs tied down. Tom's terrified eyes meet yours and you see him mouth the words, "Help me. Please!"

A man in robes steps forward and begins to slide a knife across Tom's throat.

"Nooooo!" you scream, reaching out.

Turn to page 2.

2

You lunge forward. But the only thing you clasp is the lamp next to your bed. You jerk awake and sit up, looking around. You are home in your own room. There's no altar. No singing men. You take some deep breaths. It was just a bad dream.

Three days ago, your best friend Tom disappeared on assignment in Mexico. He was doing a piece for cable TV on the ancient Mayan temples at Chichen Itza. His assistant Amanda called to tell you the news.

"Tom was onto a hot story. But he wouldn't say what on the phone. After he was reported missing, the police found fresh blood on the altar used for human sacrifice by the Mayans. No one has seen him since," Amanda tells you.

"Who called to tell you?" you ask.

"Tom's guide Manuel. Tom said that if anything happened to him, I should call you right away," she replies. "Do you think you could go down there to look for him? I'm really worried."

Go on to the next page.

Tom is your oldest friend. You have known each other since kindergarten. You have no choice; you must go to Mexico to find him.

"Of course I will go," you tell Amanda.

That was three days ago. You look at the packed bag next to your bed and then at your watch. Even though it's still dark, it's almost time to get up anyway.

A few short hours later, you are flying at 35,000 feet, en route to Merida, the capital of the Yucatan. Several books on the Mayans are spread out in front of you.

At one time, the Mayans controlled huge ceremonial, agricultural and trading centers throughout the Yucatan Peninsula of Mexico. Their kingdom stretched from Tulum, on the edge of the Caribbean Sea, to Tikal deep in the south, and on to Chichen Itza and Uxmal farther inland. Then, simply and mysteriously, the great Mayan cities faded into nothing. They became ghost towns and ruins. Mayan culture disappeared overnight. Today, vines and jungle brush cover everything.

Turn to page 5.

Tom flew into Merida. Your plan is to go there first and try to retrace Tom's steps. Amanda has arranged for Manuel, Tom's guide, to meet you at the airport.

"Manuel is a well-known guide for those who seek the mysteries of the Mayans," Amanda tells you. "And he has good connections at Merida University, where the best Mayan scholars work. But Manuel also has a reputation for being unusual. Tom suspected that he might be the reincarnation of an ancient Mayan shaman," she warns.

Your guidebooks say shamans were extremely powerful, priest-like magicians or spellbinders. The Mayans believed shamans represented the link between heaven and earth. They were the human link to Mayan gods, such as the dreaded Plumed Serpent or the enormously powerful Jaguar.

You are curious to meet this Manuel!

Turn to page 6.

Several hours later, you land at Merida and pass through Customs. Suddenly, as if appearing out of nowhere, a man is by your side.

"Hello, my name is Manuel. I am to be your guide. Welcome to Mexico." He shakes your hand, and smiles. Manuel's skin shines like copper. His large nose and sloping forehead remind you of the ancient Mayan paintings and stone carvings in the books you studied on the plane. Suddenly you realize that Manuel himself must have descended from the Mayan people. The civilization, many say, collapsed 800 years ago, but its people live on to this day.

"I tried to help Tom," Manuel says, grabbing your heaviest suitcase. "But . . . unfortunately, he did not always take my advice. Maybe together we can find him?"

"Where do you think we should start, Manuel?" you ask.

"Perhaps at the university? Dr. Lopez might help. He is a leading expert on Mayan sacrifice. Or maybe we should go straight to Chichen Itza, the last place Tom was seen alive?"

If you decide to visit Dr. Lopez, turn to page 7.

If you decide to go right to Chichen Itza, turn to page 38.

Manuel smiles with satisfaction at your choice.

"Very good. You will like Dr. Lopez. Come with me."

A taxi takes you through the narrow streets of Merida, past Spanish-style buildings and to the university. Dr. Lopez has an office on the fourth floor of a building with long hallways and high ceilings. You enter his cluttered office and he speaks.

"Welcome to the land of the Mayans," Dr. Lopez says with a smile. He waves his arm about the room. Just as you are thinking that you would be grounded if your bedroom were as messy as Dr. Lopez's office, you notice that it's crammed with Mayan art. You are looking at an amazing collection of pottery and stone carvings. There are snakes, monkeys, jaguars and fierce-looking half-human, half-animal forms. Even in the age of computer animation, the ancient Mayan icons are still powerful and menacing, you think.

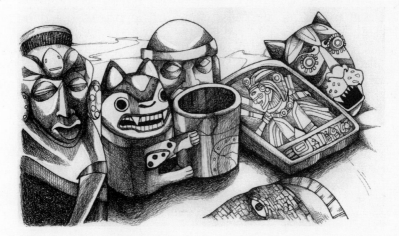

Turn to page 8.

"You are here about your friend, the young American TV reporter, aren't you?" Dr. Lopez says in a kind voice.

"Yes. Yes, I am. Can you help?"

"Perhaps," Dr. Lopez replies. "He came here and asked for information. The mystery of the Mayans has lured many. Tom is not the only one to disappear. He was keen to learn so I offered him a special and dangerous approach."

"What was that?" you ask. The hair on your neck and arms is rising. Something is afoot.

"A time-travel potion developed by the Mayans hundreds and hundreds of years ago. I gave Tom a bottle of it before he left for the site at Chichen Itza. The potion works best if you take it near one of the ancient pyramids. My guess is that your friend used it and has yet to return. I cannot explain the fresh blood on the stone altar at El Castillo, the largest pyramid there. If Tom did something to anger the Mayan priests, the blood might be his. When angry, the priests could be vicious and brutal."

"So what can we do?" you cry.

Go on to the next page.

Dr. Lopez reaches into his desk and pulls out a small flask. He holds it out toward you.

"Here. Take this. It is the last of my supply. This potion will let you travel back 800 years, to the time when Mayan civilization began to disappear. But remember. Don't show fear when you get there. You must be brave. Manuel will go with you."

Dr. Lopez nods toward your guide. You look at Manuel, who looks back. His eyes are filled with kindness. "I will go with you if you want me to," he says gently.

If you decide to take the potion and travel back in time to look for Tom, turn to page 11.

If you decline the potion, and go out to the ruins at Chichen Itza instead to talk to the local police, turn to page 38.

SECRET ONLINE ENDING

If you accept the potion, but cautiously drink only half to begin with, go to www.cyoa.com/maya24212.htm

You decide to try the time-travel potion. First, you and Manuel take a bus to Chichen Itza. When you arrive, you find a quiet corner and pull out Dr. Lopez's flask. The time travel potion is thick and slimy. You take a gulp.

Suddenly you are in a busy city. Women are carrying clay pots that look heavy in their arms, while men in the green robes from your dream walk through the streets. Directly in front of you there is a large building that appears to be a temple. Manuel is beside you.

"Act normal," he whispers. "We are 1500 years back in time, at a place called Uxmal. That big building is called the Temple of the Magicians."

He shakes his head, as if to stifle a sneeze. "The potion was extra strong," he says. "We also ended up in the wrong place."

"We're in Uxmal? Did the same thing happen to Tom?" you cry.

Manuel shrugs, his eyes darting around, as if he is looking for someone.

Turn to page 12.

You follow Manuel's gaze. He is staring across at a long, low building made of yellowish stone covered with snake carvings.

A hush falls over the crowd. Five men and one woman in gold and red robes, carrying silver spears and wearing bright green feathers in their hair, emerge from the low building. They move through the crowd and start climbing the steps of the Temple.

"They are of the Priest Clan," Manuel whispers. "That is the priestess with them."

A squad of warriors carrying knives and swords fans out in the courtyard.

By now you notice others in the crowd staring at Manuel. Several people bow down low before him. They move aside as if to make room for you both to move forward. Is Manuel a shaman after all?

He smiles at you and says, "My friend, you may choose to go with the priests and priestess or you can go with the warriors. Either group might know about how to find Tom."

You hear a horrible scream coming from a small hut behind one of the pyramids. Everyone stops.

"What was that?" you whisper.

"You will soon find out. It might be someone preparing for services. Decide now," Manuel replies in a hurried whisper.

If you decide to go with the priests and priestess, turn to page 34.

If you decide to go with the warriors, turn to page 40.

The snakebite hurts. The Plumed Serpent becomes a simple dangerous snake again. It slides over the tree trunk, tucks its head in a hole and vanishes.

It's all over. The Toltecs leave you on the spot to die. You are useless to them now.

But you don't die! The Plumed Serpent was protecting you all along. The spirit of the Plumed Serpent makes you well again. And you live on as one of the attendants of the most powerful of the Mayan gods. Perhaps you will find Tom, perhaps not.

The End

You stare at the priests in front of you. Two of them glare at you. One of them fingers his knife, and suddenly you are frightened.

The head priest looks stern and says, "Be calm, we will not hurt you. Look in the heavens. There is Venus. It is both the morning and the evening star. Venus will

guide you as it guides us. Stay with us and learn about the secrets of the universe. Learn of heaven and hell; learn of the power of the four corners of the earth."

You hesitate, but decide to stay with this group of people. Three of the priests move forward suddenly and grasp your arms. They shove you toward the blood spattered altar. Are they going to sacrifice you?

One of them speaks. "You must make a sacrifice to seal your pact with us.

There is no turning back. Here is the knife. You must cut out the heart of the victim."

You are horrified. What is to be sacrificed? Is it an animal or a human, some poor slave or prisoner from a battle? If you refuse, will they sacrifice you?

If you agree to perform a sacrifice, turn to page 65.

If you refuse, turn to page 42.

You turn to run, stumbling down the steps.

"Capture that one!" the priests scream to the warriors in the courtyard. They point at you. Everyone below looks up. Suddenly, a door in the stone steps swings open. A young woman dressed in bright green with yellow beads about her throat motions you inside.

"I am Zama, Manuel's friend. Follow me. Be quick!"

You dart inside and slam the stone door shut. It is a dark, musty tunnel that slants down into the heart of the pyramid. You follow Zama as she leads you through an underground maze. The sounds of the shouting crowd grow faint. After fifteen minutes, the two of you climb a small staircase and lift a trap door. You are somewhere in the jungle outside the Temple of Magicians. You can hear the screams of priests' victims in the distance.

"What's going on?" you ask.

"Manuel is the head of a secret group that opposes the priests. We want to stop the sacrifices and throw the priests out."

"Where are we going?"

"Kabah. It is a village nearby. You will be hidden in the old temple," Zama replies.

Go on to the next page.

It takes the rest of the day and night to get to Kabah. By nightfall, your feet are sore and blistered from walking on the sandy rock path. Once you arrive in Kabah, you see that the main temple is covered with carvings of the rain god, Chac. Zama hides you in a dark room where you are fed a meal of maize, squash, and hot chili peppers. At last you can rest. But you feel the keen edge of fear even as you sleep.

And you still have no sign of Tom!

Turn to page 18.

At dawn, an old man comes and sits before you. With a start, you recognize Dr. Lopez. He speaks.

"My friend, you now see part of the reason for the collapse of the Mayans: evil priests, fear, human sacrifices gone out of control, death."

"But what now, Dr. Lopez?"

"You can stay on in Kabah and live and work as a farmer until it is safe. Or you can go to Cozumel, an island off the coast. The journey to the island will be dangerous, but once you are there, the priests will not find you. Here at Kabah you are fairly safe as long as you do as we say. Zama will help you here."

"But where is Tom?" you ask.

"We cannot tell you . . . now," is the reply.

If you decide to stay in Kabah, turn to page 19.

If you decide to go to Cozumel, turn to page 31.

You decide to stay in Kabah. Dr. Lopez invites you to live in his small thatched-roof hut. The rhythm of life in the village is slow. You help the other villagers clear the jungle and plant small gardens. You tend the fire some nights and listen as the old ones tell stories under the stars.

Sometimes you and Dr. Lopez talk about the Mayans' way of life.

"The land here is not very good for farming. There is not much water. We cut down the jungle, and burn the brush in order to plant in the earth."

"But there is so little jungle here. What happened to it?" you ask.

"After six or seven years, the sun dries the earth and the plants take the minerals and nutrients from the soil. Then, the plants can't grow and so we must cut more jungle and burn more brush. The land we leave gets hard and unworkable. This has been going on for hundreds of years."

"I don't get it," you admit.

"The people worship the rain god, Chac," Dr. Lopez explains. "Chac has been good to them, but one day perhaps he will not be, and then the crops will fail."

"What other gods are there?"

Go on to the next page.

20

"Oh, Plumed Serpent, the ruler of all. We call him *Quetzacoatl*. And Smoking Mirror, the god of wrath. There are others too. The good and evil are intertwined. Human sacrifice is seen as a passage to greatness. Death and life are but two sides of the same shell. Your friend Tom was fascinated by the Overworld and the Otherworld. Perhaps he transited to the Otherworld, the dark side."

"Tom?" you ask. "Do you know where he is? How can I reach him?" you ask.

"You can't. You must wait. Only time will, or can, release him," Dr. Lopez replies sadly. "Tom was more intrigued by the priests than you seemed to be."

"What should I do?" you ask.

"You have been safe here so far. But you can leave for the coast if you prefer. Life along the coast is more active. Fishermen are a social bunch and many people pass through. Perhaps someone will have heard or seen your friend."

You look around. Weeks have passed. Life is pleasant but the purpose of your journey is unfinished.

If you decide to stay in Kabah, hoping Tom turns up, turn to page 23.

If you decide to leave for the coast and pursue the life of a seafaring trader, turn to page 32.

You are the mighty ruler, inheritor of the Plumed Serpent. Beware any and all who defy you. You enter Chichen Itza triumphantly. Wherever you go, people worship and love you.

Great feasts are held in the courtyard and thousands of people join in. When the ball game is played, however, you refuse to let the losers be sacrificed. You stop all sacrifices of people and animals, replacing them with offerings of maize and squash and chili peppers. The people love you and respect you, but the priests grow sullen and angry. They dislike you because you have taken away their power. Beware. The revenge of Mayan priests and shamans could be swift and terrible.

The End

As he walks away, Manuel turns to you and motions with a small rod. A beam of light shoots out of it. Suddenly you are so frightened that the hair on the back of your neck stands up and goose bumps appear on your arms. The beam of light is like an eraser and it wipes your mind clear of all memory of the day. Your last image is of a smiling Tom aboard the star cruiser.

Suddenly the spacecraft is gone and you are standing at the foot of El Castillo. You can't remember anything that happened after your breakfast with Manuel. It is quiet in the great courtyard. Your big chance has come and gone. You blew it.

The End

Kabah is rich in history and tradition. The rain god Chac adorns the walls of the temples. The Plumed Serpent is carved on most of the buildings. A girl of eleven named Mimla and a boy of fifteen named Ordex become your friends and companions. Daily you work the fields planted

with maize, squash and peppers.

In the heat of the day, you gather under the shelter of thatched roofs and play Mayan games of chance and skill called Mara Coo. The old people tell stories and recite poems about glorious leaders, bloody wars, and fierce or loving gods. You are careful to watch for the dreaded, but honored rattlesnakes, for they lurk in the dry bush ready to kill.

You grow restless and guilty that you are not searching for Tom.

"I must leave," you announce to your new friends and Dr. Lopez.

"If you stay, you could have a brilliant future as a member of our group. Soon we will overthrow the priests. You are a natural leader."

"But my friend Tom, I must find him," you state as firmly as possible.

"As you wish," is the simple answer.

Turn to page 24.

"This must be a dream-world," you say to yourself as you make the decision. "I will only find Tom in the real world . . . wherever that is."

ZAP!

Suddenly, you are standing in the same spot, but you notice a huge change. The earth has become hard from overuse. Plants can't grow. The fields are sun-scorched and brown.

The few people standing nearby stare at you. They are thin and their eyes are empty looking. No one smiles. No one greets you. There is no noise, only the sound of wind blowing in the dry bushes around the abandoned huts. There are only a few children and they, too, are quiet and unhappy. It is a sad sight.

Turn to page 26.

Dr. Lopez stands beside you. He does not smile; sadness fills his face.

"You see, the rains did not come. The earth was worn out. The crops died in the sun. You have witnessed one of the reasons for the collapse of the Mayans."

You nod your head solemnly.

"Where to next?"

Dr. Lopez says you can leave Kabah and travel on a southwesterly course to the hills and lush rainforests. Or you can follow the trail that leads back to Uxmal. You have no idea where Tom might be.

If you decide to go to the hills and rainforests, turn to page 61.

If you decide to return to Uxmal, turn to page 27.

You travel back to Uxmal. There you see mounds of green bushes and shrubs, and you realize that underneath the bushes are the temples and houses. The jungle has covered the stone buildings. It is fascinating to you that this same place was once so prosperous and filled with happy people. Now, centuries later, it is a desolate ghost town. No sounds are heard.

Then you hear it . . . the sound of a flute.

Turn to page 28.

The flute calls to you; it has a magical hold on you. Perhaps it is a siren song, coming from ancient times, used as a means of putting people into spells and trances?

Two people approach you from the edge of the jungle. Wow! It's Manuel and a friend.

"You see, the rains stopped. No crops grew. The people believed that Chac, the rain god, grew angry with them."

"What happened then? From the looks of the jungle, the rains must have come back."

Manuel answers, "Oh, the rains returned. But it was

too late. By that time the people had moved on. They stopped believing in the power of the priests. They left in search of better land and more water. The people believed that Chac had cursed the area."

"I understand this," you say, "but what happened to Tom? Did you show him this too?"

"I cannot tell you. You must search on your own."

The End

If you would like to start your investigation over again, turn to page 38.

Both Dr. Lopez and Zama tell you of the clear water and the white beaches, and your mind is made up. Perhaps Tom followed the same escape route you did, and he is waiting for you on the beach. Either way, you've got to get away from the priests with blood in their hair. For ten days you struggle through the jungle with Zama. Thorns and dry branches tear your clothes and skin. Poisonous snakes are a constant danger; the sounds of their rattles the only warning of their deadly presence. But snakes are nothing compared to the occasional glimpses of jaguars! Finally, the jungle brush thins and the path you are on enters sparse grasslands. The smell of the ocean fills the air.

You stand on the shore, feet in the water, letting the sand run through your toes. At a small fishing village, you board a boat headed for Cozumel.

A sudden squall hits. Great waves smash against the small boat. It fills with water and begins to sink. Salt water fills your mouth, and a strange thing happens. The salt water washes away the effects of the magic potion.

You find yourself in the present again. You have forgotten all about your visit to Dr. Lopez and your trip to the past. You do remember that finding Tom is your mission.

Turn to page 38.

You head for the coast on foot and arrive on the island of Cozumel after four days of travel by boat. Cozumel is a paradise. Coral reefs are filled with fish. Giant sea turtles swim near the northern end of the island, and birds fill the air at sunrise and sunset. It is hard to tell where the sea ends and the sky begins.

The island is the home of Mayan traders who travel up and down the coast exchanging cloth, jade, fish, and pottery. Perhaps they have heard of your friend. You ask around. No one has heard of Tom or seen him, until one day, a trader arrives who has heard rumors of a strange young man with white skin. He is being held captive on Isla Mujeres, the trader tells you.

If you try to get to Isla Mujeres, turn to page 85.

If you believe the people who say that the story is nonsense, turn to page 86.

The crowd parts further as you and Manuel walk after the priests and priestess. You begin to climb the steep stone steps. When you reach a ledge, the priestess watches you closely as the five priests form a tight square around you. Their long black hair is covered with a sticky evil-smelling substance. You ask Manuel what it is.

"Blood. It is the blood of the victims of the sacrifices. The priests think it makes them stronger. You will see. It is called itza!"

You pull back in horror.

"Sacrifices? What for? What kind of sacrifices?"

"Be patient. Just follow the priests. Do not show fear, whatever you do."

Manuel hangs back. The priests alongside you climb the steep steps of the Temple of the Magicians, one by one. At the top of the pyramid, there is a small room with a stone altar stained with brownish, dried blood.

"You are now going to be one of us," says the head priest, as if he's known you before. "Welcome to the Mayan priesthood, where men and women are . . ."

But he does not finish. A blood-curdling scream rises from below. What is going on?

If you decide to escape and make a run for it now, turn to page 16.

If you decide to stay and accept their offer of priest-hood, for maybe it will lead to Tom, turn to page **14**.

You try to continue on course. But gale-force winds and huge waves force your ship in an easterly direction. It is all you can do to keep the ship from swamping. One sailor is swept overboard, his screams lost in the roar of the waves.

"Captain, can't you do anything?" you scream out.

He does not answer. The wind and sea take all his attention.

For a whole day your boat is tossed about by the storm. Then, once again, the wind picks up in force. You are propelled through the seas as if your boat had a motor, instead of sails.

"Land! Land straight ahead," the look-out shouts. Then you all see it. Palm trees, white beaches, and high mountains. You have reached what someday will be called Cuba. The boat slams through the surf and grates to rest on the beach. You are met by a group of tall and bronze Arawak Indians with broad smiling faces. They are friendly and offer rest and food. They invite you to stay with them.

If you choose to stay in Cuba, turn to page 116.

If you continue with the ship back to Cancun and the trade route, turn to page 117.

You decide to go straight to Chichen Itza to talk to the police. First, you and Manuel drive to your hotel in Merida to spend the night. Merida was founded by the Spanish after their conquest of Mexico in the sixteenth century. Their old churches and fortresses give the town a Spanish flavor.

"Tomorrow we begin," Manuel says. "Chichen Itza, the largest site of Mayan ruins, is famous as a center of lost power. It holds a huge pyramid, a domed observatory, a deep water hole or *cenote*, and the famed and feared ball court. In ancient times, the losers of the ball game also lost their lives.

That night, you notice that Manuel is quiet. He clears his throat to speak. "I have been thinking," Manuel begins. "You may want to go to Uxmal first. While smaller than Chichen Itza, Uxmal is far older. The Temple of the Magicians at Uxmal is filled with mystery.

"That last day, Tom kept it a secret where he went," Manuel adds.

If you decide to go to Chichen Itza first, turn to page 46.

If you decide go to Uxmal instead, turn to page 44.

You drew yellow. It is the straw of the ruler. You are immediately made the new ruler of the Toltecs. You rule until you die of old age at 93. Several times Manuel and Dr. Lopez try to get you to go back to the present, but you refuse. You enjoy being the ruler.

The End

The warriors are practicing fighting maneuvers with bow and arrow, spear, and club. They are a noisy group, bragging and shouting, punching and wrestling.

Manuel tells you these warriors have come from Chichen Itza. He introduces you to the officer in charge. On your way back to Chichen Itza, the officer speaks to you.

"There are two groups here. One group raids our enemies to get slaves or take revenge. The slaves are used for sacrifice. The soldiers in that unit are fast, quiet in the jungle, and ready to die if captured.

"The other group defends us against invaders. They are careful and watchful. They never give up. They will fight until the last one is dead."

Turn to page 43.

42

"No!" you shout, "I will never sacrifice a living being to any god for any reason. You are all crazy."

It was a mistake to say that. The priests become very quiet and solemn. The sun is bright in the sky. Manuel is nowhere to be seen. The sound of a bird breaks the quiet as two of the priests move toward you. They are not smiling. One says, "Since you will not perform the sacrifice, we will. You will be the victim."

The End

"Who are your enemies?" you ask.

"Toltecs, a savage group who worships Smoking Mirror, their god of war and death. They are always invading us." Several warriors nod in agreement.

The officer in command says, "It's up to you. You can go on raids or stay here in defense."

If you decide to join the raiding party,
turn to page 48.

If you choose to stay, turn to page 49.

You've got a hunch that Tom might have gone to Uxmal. You go with Manuel to the bus station for the trip there. The trip is long and hot, but finally you arrive at the ruins of the city. The Temple of the Magicians looms over the land. Steep stone steps ascend to a smaller temple building on top of the pyramid. Across from the Temple of the Magicians is a large, rectangular

building which the Spanish Conquistadors called the Nunnery. No one really knows what it was used for.

"What do you think, Manuel? Any ideas about its purpose?" you ask.

Manuel hesitates for a minute and says, "Perhaps the building was the palace of the Shamans. Maybe they conducted their magic there."

Where should you start looking, at the Temple of the Magicians or the Nunnery? What would Tom have done if he had come to Uxmal?

If you investigate the Temple of the Magicians, turn to page 50.

If you investigate the Nunnery, turn to page 52.

The highway to Chichen Itza runs through flat, scrubby land. A few houses or huts line the road. Then you see a giant form on the horizon. It grows larger and larger as your bus approaches, until the bus stops for good in the monument's shadow. El Castillo, the giant pyramid, looms above you.

Broad avenues lead out from the pyramid to other stone buildings, to courtyards, and to the evil ball court where Mayans lost their lives if they lost the game. One avenue leads to the *cenote*, or giant well, which has taken the bodies of many sacrificial victims.

A group of twenty people stand quietly at the base of El Castillo.

Your eyes follow a finger pointing up into the sky. The top of the pyramid is glowing with a bright red color! Where is it coming from?

A large spacecraft hovers over the pyramid.

"What does it mean, Manuel? What's happen-ing?" You are frightened.

"These Mayan ruins are contact points for other planets. That group of people has been asked to leave Earth for the planet Merganatic."

You believe in UFOs, but now that you are seeing one, it is frightening.

"Manuel, this is incredible. Why is that thing here?"

Go on to the next page.

"Earth is seen as a leading planet. Other civilizations want to learn from us. They send emissaries to ask us to return with them to an outergalactic congress on the rights of life in the universe. That is the last group of people attending the congress to depart. If you think Tom may have gone on the mission, you should join them."

Is Manuel making this up? There is no denying the bright red glow on top of the pyramid.

If you decide to join the mission, knowing the danger of never returning, turn to page 62.

If you decide to stay and finish your job, turn to page 64.

You want to see action, but are you prepared to fight? It's one thing to travel in time; it's quite something else to be a warrior involved in real fighting. You could never kill anybody. And what if you have to defend yourself? Still, you decide to join the raids.

After three weeks of training, the warrior chief says, "OK, now it is time. You will go on a raid to Itxal, three days from here."

If you join in the fighting, turn to page 67.

If you decide to watch from a hiding place, turn to page 68.

You stay in Chichen Itza. The days are pleasant and you make good friends among the young Mayan warriors. Your desire to find Tom fades, but you vow to keep a sharp look-out.

The Mayans are farmers, traders, craftsmen, and warriors. Settlements of houses spread out from Chichen Itza and Uxmal. In this crowded land, water is scarce.

Some of the people tend to the fields while others work making cotton cloth for trading with other Mayan centers. People come to Chichen Itza for great ceremonies, to trade, and to have their disputes settled by the priests or nobles.

One day, several of the warriors come together. A tall man with broad shoulders speaks.

"Would you like to play the ball game?" he asks.

He explains the game and shows you the court and the hard rubber ball. The object is to get the ball through the carved stone hoop. The game looks fast and difficult and the man tells you it takes much skill, and that the teams that play in the great ball court on ceremonial days face a real test. If they win, they are heroes; but if they lose, they are used as sacrifices in the ceremonies that follow.

They say that the ball game represents the struggle between Lords of Life and Lords of Death.

You are selected to join one of the teams.

If you refuse to play, turn to page 70.

If you decide to play, turn to page 72.

50

The words "Temple of the Magicians" excite you. You walk toward the huge pyramid, but a crowd of tourists is busy snapping cameras and pushing and shoving. They surround the base.

You stand for a moment waiting for the crowd to clear, when an old man with wrinkled skin wearing the colorful shawl of the Mayans shuffles up to you.

"Come with me," he says, beckoning with a hand crippled with age. "I will take you to see a very deep water hole, a secret *cenote*. Water is scarce in this dry land and the *cenotes* are the most important reasons for choosing a place to live. Without water, there is no chance to live. You will be amazed at what I will show you at this *cenote*."

You look around, but Manuel is nowhere to be seen. Where has he gone?

If you decide to go with the old man,
turn to page 71.

If you decline and decide to wait for Manuel,
turn to page 76.

The building called the Nunnery is intricately designed with carvings of birds, snakes, and humanlike creatures. There are few clues as to what the building was used for. The rooms are too dark to have been used for living quarters.

Poking around in a dark room with a flashlight, you see a piece of white paper stuck to the far wall. It says:

Hotel Maya, Chichen Itza, Room 927
Thursday night
You must come. There is danger.

You puzzle over the note. It is Thursday. Is this note for you? How could it be? What should you do? A figure moves quickly from an adjoining room. Did that person follow you and leave the note?

*If you decide to go to the Hotel Maya,
turn to page 75.*

*If you ignore the note and go on to another room,
turn to page 77.*

The priests wait impatiently as you ramble on about not wanting to kill anyone. Their eyes gleam and their bodies shake as though with fever.

"You must do it," one of them shouts at you. "You must!"

"But it isn't right. I can't kill. I won't kill."

One of the priests lunges at you, but you duck to one side. He tumbles down the steps of the temple. The crowd of people standing below look up in horror. In the confusion, you sneak down the other side of the pyramid. Although the steps are extremely steep, you make it and manage to lose yourself in the crowd. You ask a man where the warriors can be found. He points to the courtyard. You decide to join them. Nothing can be more warlike than life with the priests. Perhaps the warriors will be more civilized.

Turn to page 40.

56

You follow the path hoping you're going in the right direction. At first you feel as though your lungs might burst from running so hard. Then you feel the muscles in your legs begin to tighten. You don't think you can take another step. A root catches your foot, and you fall forward. The last thing you remember is the earth rushing toward you. You black out.

When you come to, you examine your head and arms and legs. Everything is all right except for a bump on your forehead. Your mouth is dry and your tongue feels swollen.

You call out, "Anybody there?" Maybe that's a dumb thing to do. The enemy could be nearby and might hear you.

If you continue to call for help, turn to page 89.

If you decide to lie still and rest while you gather strength, turn to page 90.

"So, you thought you could escape, did you? You are perfect for our next sacrifice to the rain god." It is the enemy chief talking. You have been captured.

An old priestess with deep wrinkles on her face rushes up to you and says, "No, we don't need a sacrifice. We need a slave to work for us in the temple. This prisoner will do." Her name is Muscla and she has a great deal of power, for the chief listens to her and agrees.

"Take this pest, do what you wish! We'll catch others."

Later that day you are put into a dark room in the back of a small temple. It smells of wood smoke. As you enter you notice the imprint of a hand—a red hand—on the wall. You have read about this symbol, but what does it mean?

Then a strange thing begins to happen. Your vision blurs and musical notes fill the air. When you reach out to touch the wall, you feel dizzy and begin to stumble. That's it! The potion is wearing off. You are on your way back to the present.

If you would like to try investigating in Chichen Itza, turn to page 38.

Tracking the jaguar isn't easy. The cat is sly and moves quietly through the bush. After stalking it, you understand why the Mayans worship the Jaguar. It is one of their important gods. You think it is because the cat seems to have supernatural powers. You try to guess what its next move will be. Whenever you think the cat is ahead of you, it suddenly appears behind you or off

to the side. Maybe the jaguar is tracking you? You become so absorbed in the pursuit that you lose all track of time and place. You yell for Xha, but he's nowhere to be found. You don't know where to go or where to turn. You are lost!

Then you hear sounds of people talking. None of them are Xha. They might be friends or they might be a band of enemy raiders. You hide behind some bushes and wait and watch.

Turn to page 93.

Your thirst wins out. You and Xha follow an old, unused path that winds between low-lying hills and thickets. The path ends abruptly at a *cenote*.

You feel an overwhelming impulse to take a swim. "Come on, Xha," you cry, as you plunge into the cool, fresh water. Under the surface, you see a round opening so you swim toward it. It could either be a man-made tunnel or a natural cave. You come out into a huge underground cavern. In the corner of the cavern lies a pile of treasure: glittering gold, jade rings of the deepest green, and plates of silver, gold and jade. It is beautiful beyond your wildest imagination.

Coming back up for air you tell Xha what you saw, and both of you descend, and enter the tunnel.

"Wow, it's the lost treasure of the Plumed Serpent!" says Xha.

You stare at this treasure in amazement. You want to claim it.

Do you try to take this gold now? If so, turn to page 96.

If you decide to return to modern times to collect this fabulous treasure, turn to page 97.

You have heard people speak of the hill country to the south. They tell stories of a great rain forest, large temples, pyramids and rich soil. They also speak of warfare. People from the west have been raiding the prosperous towns in the south in search of prisoners and treasure.

You set out with a guide toward the fabled hills in the south. For days you travel under the blistering sun. Water is scarce, and your food runs out. After awhile you begin to doubt that your guide knows where he is going. You wish you knew more about astronomy so that you could use the stars to guide the way. You grow weaker and weaker from lack of food and water. After almost eight days you can barely walk. You must have some water. But there is none.

You are never seen or heard from again. Your last thoughts are that this is probably what happened to Tom.

The End

One by one, the group standing at the pyramid enters the spacecraft by the transporter beam. You notice that halfway to the spacecraft, their bodies begin to glow. No one seems to be afraid.

Gaining confidence, you step into the transporter beam and are carried up into the spacecraft. You hear nothing as you shoot up and away into the far reaches of the universe, to the planet Merganatic and the great Congress on Intergalactic Life. You wonder why the Mayan sites were chosen as contact points. Their brutal and complex society seems an odd choice for other planets. Who knows what lies ahead?

The End

You laugh out loud and point at the spacecraft and the people entering it.

"Great show, Manuel, great show! Tell me, how did you do it? What is it, the set for some movie?"

Manuel does not smile and does not speak. He shakes his head and moves off to join the group who are going up the transporter beam into the spacecraft.

Turn to page 22.

"Yes, I will perform the sacrifice," you whisper.

"Speak up, we can't hear you," the priest with the knife yells at you.

"Yes, I will do the sacrifice, but what for?" You try to hide your fear, but you can't.

The head priest steps forward and says to you, "Water is scarce, so we sacrifice to the god, Chac, for rain. Crops die in the fields. Sickness takes our people. War ruins us. Each time we sacrifice, we hope the gods will treat us better and keep us from harm."

"But," you say, "what can killing someone or something do? I mean, it's crazy."

Turn to the next page.

"No more talk. Act. Take the knife. Bring the sacrifice to Chac." The priestess points to the altar.

A slave holding a chicken climbs the temple steps. Behind him, two soldiers lead a prisoner kicking and screaming. Looking into the prisoner's eyes, you see the fear of death and the pleading to be saved.

What can you do?

If you accept the knife, turn to page 80.

If you stall for time, turn to page 54.

You travel by foot through the jungle to Ixtal. Your attack is a complete success. The element of surprise works very well, and your band had the upper hand from the first. Even the chickens and dogs belonging to the villagers ran for cover. Dust rose as you raced around. A large group of people led by a woman escaped into the surrounding jungle, but you and your band let them go.

You return triumphant, happy that no one was killed or hurt. Back in Chichen Itza, Manuel welcomes you and says, "So, you like leading the life of a Mayan. Well, I'm not surprised. Your friend, Tom, did not like it. He paid the supreme price."

The End

You watch the fighting from behind a bush. Off to the right you see three of the enemy pulling on a large hemp rope. It releases a bent tree. The tree has a bucket filled with rocks that shower down on you.

"Watch out!" you scream. "Duck!"

Two of your warriors are knocked out. A flurry of arrows and spears fills the air. Three more of your warriors are wounded. Shouts and screams pierce the air.

"Escape!" your captain yells.

The attack is a complete failure. The enemy had more strength and courage than you ever imagined.

When you try to retreat, you become confused. Where do you go? You are cut off from the other warriors.

*If you follow a path that leads from the clearing,
turn to page 56.*

If you decide to stay put, turn to page 57.

"I'm not playing that game," you say. "Find another sucker. Those are the craziest rules I've ever heard. No way. Lose and you die?"

Several of the warriors nod in agreement, but most of them like the idea of being heroes if they win. The thought of death doesn't frighten them as much as it does you. Some say that it is considered an honor to be sacrificed to a god. Not for you though.

A young warrior, Xha, suggests a hunt for a jaguar that has been seen near the maize fields instead. You agree to go.

The day is hot, and the track of the jaguar is hard to follow. By late afternoon you are far from the maize and squash fields. Without your friends, you would be lost. You are almost out of water and night is coming on.

If you choose to search for water with Xha,
turn to page 60.

If you go with Xha after the jaguar, turn to page 58.

You have always been an adventurer, so of course you follow the old man to the secret *cenote*. The trail is a faint path through the tangle of bushes, and within fifteen minutes you are completely lost.

"Hey, old man, where is this *cenote* of yours?"

He turns and smiles at you.

"Here it is."

But instead of a *cenote*, you find yourself surrounded by three men. One of them holds a gun, and the other two have knives. They do not smile.

"Give us your money."

You fumble for your wallet. There are two American ten-dollar bills and 300 Mexican pesos. You hand them over to the men. They tie you up with a rough hemp rope, load you onto a donkey, and move off into the jungle.

"We will hold you for ransom. Your people will pay and pay plenty. If they don't, you die. We have another hostage, you will keep him company."

You hope that your family will be able to come up with the ransom money. You also hope that the other hostage is Tom.

The End

Before you know it, you are on the field in the ball court. Shouting fills the air as the two teams practice. A large crowd gathers to watch.

Six priests, three elders, and a group dressed in clothes of golden cloth march in, take their honored places, and signal for the game to begin.

What if you lose? Your eyes quickly travel to the steps of the pyramid called El Castillo. You have heard of victims having their hearts ripped out and then being thrown down the steps into the courtyard.

The game is long and hard. The score is close. Your heart pounds. With loud screams and yells, a raiding party bursts into the ball court. They are Toltecs, a tribe of fierce warriors from the north and west. You run off

the ball court and hide in the bushes next to the big *cenote*. Others are not so lucky and die in agony.

The Toltecs fan out and hunt for survivors. As you try to escape, you are spotted and chased. Your heart is pounding, you feel as though life is already over. Tom appears out of nowhere.

"Come with me . . . now!" he shouts. You join him and run through a stone arch. Suddenly you are back in the present.

"Tell me, Tom, was this true what we did?" you gasp.

"As true as true gets," he replies.

The End

Who put the note in the darkened room? Who could have known you would be there and would find it? It might well be the secret forces of the Mayans at work—forces too hidden for most humans to understand. You are fascinated.

You check into the Hotel Maya. At nine o'clock when you walk down the corridor to Room 327, soldiers leap out of Rooms 328 and 329 and arrest you. They are all heavily armed. You can smell the oil on the weapons. Their captain speaks to you in Spanish, but then switches to English when you don't reply.

"So, you are the spy we have been waiting for. We knew we would catch you. If you are wondering what happened to your friend in Room 327, I'll tell you. He was captured two days ago, and is now in jail. You revolutionaries are all the same."

The captain orders the soldiers to take you away under arrest.

If you plead innocence, turn to page 83.

If you tell the truth, turn to page 84.

You ignore the old man. Who knows what he is after?

As you walk away from him, a rock with a piece of paper wrapped around it drops at your feet. You look up, startled, but you see no one who could have dropped this rock.

The paper contains a short message that says:

RETURN TO THE NUNNERY.
MEET WITH US IN
THE SEVENTH ROOM

The message is signed with a red handprint.

What should you do? Manuel is walking back toward you. You rush over and show him the note. Manuel looks at the note and shakes his head.

"Leave it alone. It could be dangerous."

If you decide to ignore Manuel's advice and go to the Nunnery, turn to page 81.

If you decide to ignore the instructions in the note and go instead to the Mexican police, turn to page 78.

Don't like taking chances, do you? OK, go ahead. The next room is small and as dark as the others. You step cautiously into the room. Suddenly the floor beneath you gives way and you fall into a bright blue space, gathering speed at the rate of 32 feet per second. The rush of air against you flattens your nose against your face, slicks your hair back, and squishes your lips.

The trap door opened onto a chute into the very heart of the Nunnery. Three levels below ground lies a secret ceremonial chamber where magic was conducted. Now you are but a participant in a great ancient Mayan ceremony.

The End

You see two policeman near the tourist buses.

"We're sorry but we can't help you. We are too busy. We are trying to find one of your countrymen who vanished several weeks ago."

You show them the note. When they see the sign of the red hand, they become very excited.

"Wait! Just one minute. Don't leave. Stay right there."

They talk in hushed tones, and then they radio their headquarters.

"The captain is coming right away."

Soon you hear the whirring of a helicopter. When it lands in the courtyard, three men get out.

"Let me see the note." It is the captain speaking. He is a heavy man with a black mustache.

"Aha! I see. The red hand. This is the mark of the revolutionaries. How did you come by this note? Do you know the American named Tom?"

If you cooperate with the police, turn to page 98.

If you just want to get out of this mess of the "red hand", turn to page 99.

80

Human sacrifices! Throughout history, people have been sacrificed to appease gods. Fortunately, this time it is the chicken that is to be sacrificed. Even so, the very idea of drawing the stone knife across the chicken's throat and watching its lifeblood flow onto the altar gives you the creeps.

You decide to try and bring an end to this needless sacrifice. Perhaps, if you volunteer to work with the prisoners who are to be sacrificed, you will be able to devise a plan to help them escape. Time is running out, because the ceremony of sacrifice is only three weeks away. Maybe Tom is being held prisoner here.

If you plan to escape, turn to page 87.

If you call in Manuel and plead for help, turn to page 88.

The red handprint is ominous. What can it mean?

You enter the seventh room in the Nunnery building. Although it is dark inside, you see a face. It is luminous, and glows with a soft, yellowish light. A person clothed in silver with golden armbands stands in the middle of the room.

"You and three others have been chosen to journey to far space. Uxmal is our earth base. Join us if you have the courage. The earth as we know it will no longer be safe."

You listen in amazement to all that he says. It sounds like the prediction made by Mayan priests hundreds and hundreds of years ago. It is scary, because maybe they were right.

Tom suddenly appears, and it is clear he has already been to space and back. "Come with us," he tells you. "It is time."

You decide to go with them.

The End

"Captain, it's all a mistake. I was on my way to my own room. I just came to this room by mistake. I am no revolutionary or spy. You must believe me."

The captain laughs. "They all say that. You are all the same. Spies, radicals, thieves. We have a way to deal with you!"

You are handcuffed, put into a jeep and driven to Merida. There, you are thrown into a small, damp, evil-smelling cell in the local jail. The captain comes to see you the next day to tell you that the judge has given you a 30-year sentence for plotting to overthrow the government.

"But I've had no trial," you protest.

"We caught you red-handed, and we don't believe in trials anyway. These are dangerous times. You can call this the Revenge of the Mayans. You have angered their ancient gods!" he laughs.

He stubs out a cigarette in the earthen floor, sticks his short, brown hands in his pockets, and walks away from your cell. You grab the bars of the cell and scream for help. Three guards at the end of the corridor just laugh. You will be in jail for a long time.

The End

"But Captain, this is all a mistake. I am here to find a lost friend. I am no spy."

The captain leads you into a room where three men are seated at a table. They look up when you enter. The thin one says, "Wrong person! Who is this? That's not the one we want."

The man says, "Let the prisoner go. We are just wasting valuable time. The spy has had warning and time to escape."

Is Tom the "spy" they are talking about?

"As for you, we have decided to deport you," the captain adds.

"Deport me? But what about my friend Tom?" you cry.

"Tom will have to take care of himself," is the stern reply.

The End

You arrange to get to Isla Mujeres by giving your watch to a ship captain.

"Come along then. We are leaving right away," the captain says after you hand over your watch.

You cast off, and later that day, as the boat cuts through the water, you see black storm clouds gathering to the east.

"Captain, looks like a blow coming."

"The storms here are fierce." Suddenly the water is savage, a deadly dark green color.

All crew members are called on deck. But the storm breaks fast. Vicious waves pound the hull, and gale-force winds rip at the sails. The waves try to wrench the tiller from your hands. The rough water stings your eyes and drenches your clothes.

The captain asks you what you want to do.

If you want to continue on course, despite the storm, turn to page 37.

If you decide to head toward land, turn to page 102.

You don't believe Tom has been out here in Cozumel. It's your instinct. In fact, you're beginning to feel that your search for Tom is a lost cause. But . . . maybe you should check out Tulum down the coast before giving up entirely . . .

If you decide to go to Tulum, turn to page 100.

If you decide to go back to the ship, turn to page 104.

Escape from the temple is a problem. Guards are alert to any noise or movement. But the warrior prisoners from other cities in the Mayan world know that it is their only chance. They don't want to be sacrificed to the Lords of Death in the Underworld.

Together, you wait until nightfall. Only the sound of insects fills the air. You creep forward, overpower two guards and spread out into the darkened courtyard of the temple.

The escape is a success! The guards were easy to overpower. Maybe they don't really believe in sacrifices either? Could it be that only the priests want the sacrifices in order to control the people by fear? The terrible beauty of Mayan beliefs is not for everyone.

If you raise a revolt against the priests, turn to page 106.

If you decide that it is time to escape once and for all and get back to modern times, turn to page 107.

"Manuel, help! I didn't bargain for this."

Once again your mysterious friend appears.

He holds out his clenched fists for you to make your choice. "Choose the right hand or the left hand."

"What kind of choice is that, Manuel? That's just rolling dice."

Manuel looks at you long and hard. His black eyes almost burn through you.

"The choices lie deep within you. Do not hesitate. Choose now."

If you point to the right hand, turn to page 108.

If you point to the left, turn to page 109.

Your cries for help have been heard by two of your fellow warriors. They are at your side now and help you to your feet. You are groggy, but with their help you stumble on through the jungle for more than three hours. The cries of your pursuers grow fainter.

Finally you are able to stop and rest, hidden by a small rock outcropping. One of the warriors cleans out the cut on your forehead and squeezes the juices from a plant into your wound.

The three of you rest for the night, taking turns keeping a watchful eye on the surrounding jungle.

When the orange sun finally appears in the sky, you all give thanks and continue back to Chichen Itza. "My friends, without you, I would be lost. I owe my life to you."

The End

You lie on the ground feeling dizzy and sick to your stomach. The Earth spins around and the colors you see are a blur. You grip a rock in your right hand, trying to hold on. Then you faint.

When you awaken you are cold, hungry, stiff and alone. The call of an owl echoes in the jungle. Sounds of twigs snapping and dry leaves rustling seem louder than they would if you weren't frightened.

Two people appear, creeping from hiding places between first one, then another, tree. You hold your breath and don't move a muscle. They are coming toward you. You can almost feel one of their spears pushing into your back.

Turn to page 94.

You don't know who these people are or where they have come from, but talking to them is worth the risk. You couldn't survive long in this desolate area alone without food and water. You sneak toward them through the jungle, fearful of making even the slightest noise. The talking grows louder.

Peering around a clump of bushes, you see a group seated around a small fire. They are eating. The food smells good and you are very hungry. You step out from behind the tree. Before you have a chance to say anything, two men jump to their feet. Several grab their short spears. They surround you.

"Hey, I'm friendly. I'm not an enemy. I'm lost."

The leader shouts commands.

Turn to page 95.

As they get closer, you realize that the only things they are carrying in their hands are—cameras! They have been creeping around to take pictures of the rare birds in the area. Your time potion has worn off. You must have been out cold for a whole day.

Soon you are being rushed to the hospital. As you lean back in the ambulance, you smile weakly at those two kind people who have rescued you. You don't bother starting in on the story of your time travel. You know they'll never believe you.

The End

"Tie the prisoner up. Quick!"

Rough hemp rope binds your arms and legs. You are suddenly pushed to the ground. The rope bites at your wrists.

"Where are you from? Tell us or you die."

"I'm from Chichen Itza." You try to hide your trembling.

The leader smiles an evil smile.

"We are Toltecs. You Mayans are fools. We will conquer you. Now lead us to your city."

"I'm lost."

"Liar! Lead us to Chichen Itza and maybe we'll send you back north to Teotihuacan with the other prisoners." He points at a sullen group of Mayans who are tied up just as you are. You recognize Xha among them.

If you agree to try to lead them to Chichen Itza, turn to page 111.

If you refuse, turn to page 110.

The lure of gold is great. From the beginning of time people have worshiped the shiny metal. They have fought wars, plundered cities, and committed murder in its name. Some say gold has a curse on it.

You lose all track of time and place. You seat yourself in front of the treasure and feel the smooth metal. Time passes quickly, until a rumbling sound wakens you from your dreams of wealth. Rocks tumble from the roof of the cavern; boulders slide down and seal off the cave. The air grows hot. Soon the oxygen will be gone.

You are finished. Your are sealed in the cave by an earthquake. Is it the revenge of the ancient Mayans?

The End

Leaving Xha, you run as fast as you can out of the cave, and along the path back to Chichen Itza. There, you find Manuel.

"Manuel, Manuel, I want to go back to modern times. Please send me back."

Manuel studies your face. He does not smile.

"If that is your wish, it will be done. But don't be hasty."

"I want to go. Now!"

Suddenly you are in the present time, driving along a modern road built over the old path. You want to see if you can find the *cenote* where the gold was hidden in the past. When you reach the site, you park the car. Trembling with excitement, you put on a wet suit and aqualung and dive below the surface of the *cenote*.

To your horror, the entrance to the cave has been blocked. It looks like there is barely enough room for you to get in. But if you were to go for help, others will know about your discovery.

If you try to enter the cave through the small hole in the landslide, turn to page 112.

If you decide to return to the surface and go for help, turn to page 113.

At police headquarters you repeat your story. The police keep firing questions at you.

"How did you get here?"

"Why did you come here?"

"Tell us the truth."

Finally they give up the questioning. Everyone is exhausted. The captain now turns to you, stubs out his evil-smelling cigarette in the full ashtray, looks you in the eye and says, "OK." He pauses. "Are you brave? Will you agree to become a double agent? Join the revolutionary gang. Pretend to be one of them. We need information. You can help us stop this revolt."

"But how can I do it? They'll find out that I'm working for you and they'll kill me."

"That is the risk you take, but what can I say? The one named Tom agreed to help."

"Where would I start if I agree to be a double agent?"

The captain points to a map on the wall. "See, there is the island of Cancun. It's a hotbed of revolutionaries. You would go there. Or you could go to Merida. That is the headquarters of the gang. We think your friend Tom went there. But no one knows."

If you agree to go to Merida, turn to page 114.

If you agree to go to Cancun, turn to page 115.

You start to run but soon you are surrounded by angry policemen. Manuel comes up to you and whispers in your ear. "If you take this time potion now, you'll get out of this mess. Here."

He hands you a small bottle and you drink it. The police are amazed because one moment you are there and the next you are gone.

"What happened? Wh-wh-where did the prisoner go?"

It's too late. You are back in the past. They will never find you.

But, how will you ever return to the present?

The End

Tulum is a spot of terrifying beauty on a cliff above the smashing surf. You reach this ceremonial center with mysterious ease, but once there, terror overwhelms you. Plague has broken out.

*If you try to organize a medical team,
turn to page 118.*

If you decide to leave Tulum, turn to page 119.

The captain decides to head back for home port. You come about and run with the wind for the island of Cozumel, but just then, a squall hits and cracks the mast. The boat founders; the rudder is useless.

Helpless, you watch as wave after wave batters the boat. Finally, a wave four times the size of the others sweeps over the frail craft. With a wrenching crash, the boat breaks up.

You hold onto a piece of mast. It serves as a float, and after four hours you are washed ashore. You are the lone survivor. Enough of the sailor's life for you.

Gasping for breath, you call out to Manuel and ask him to bring you back to the present.

"What is it, my friend?"

"I want out. I've had enough."

"Your wish is granted."

Suddenly you are back in Merida. Was it all a dream? When you look in your brown notebook, it is full of writing.

You have not found Tom. But you have enough wild tales to write a book: of fiction.

The End

The work on board the ship is hard, but you are learning about the Mayans as you sail from town to town. They are talented potters. They weave beautiful cloth of orange and gold and brown. They carve figures of their gods. Theirs is a rich and varied culture.

Go on to the next page.

Then one day, a strange thing happens. Just as you are putting out to sea, a lookout shouts, "A mountain, a white mountain, a volcano is moving on the water." He waves and shouts frantically. There on the horizon is a large white passenger ship. Smoke is pouring out of its funnels. It is flying the Swedish flag. As it comes closer you see people lining the deck, waving and taking pictures.

You, your ship, and your friends are caught in a time warp, where parallel lines cross in space and time flip-flops back and forth. Now you are in the present but aboard your ancient craft! The other ship is a cruise ship loaded with tourists. They look at you with amusement, thinking you are just some local fishermen in a funny boat.

When you try to talk to them your voices fall into a void. The time warp is only a visual warp. There is no way out of it. You are locked in fixed time in fixed space. For eternity you ride the waves in a Mayan boat.

The End

Where do you begin? How do you start a revolt? It sounds great, but the priests are powerful. They have spies everywhere, and they are suspicious of everyone and everything. Their suspicions grow out of their greedy and evil ways. Suspected revolutionaries are quickly dragged up to a sacrificial altar and their heads are severed by a sword blow. The people tremble in fear of this group of priests.

Probably time will overcome the priests. They will grow lazy and contented, and the people will be more ready for revolt than they are now. Then revolts will happen and justice will prevail.

Meanwhile, your search for Tom is a failure. So return to the present time and try again.

The End

You are very frightened. You must get out of this place fast! You feel your entire body focused on this one desire, and then . . .

. . . suddenly you are back in Merida watching television in your hotel room. Your decision for the night is where to go out and have dinner. Still no Tom, but at least you're safe.

The End

Slowly, Manuel unclenches his right fist. Inside is a key to a safe-deposit box at the Merida airport. He smiles and says, "You are back on your way, my friend. The trip is over. You are back in the present. There is a gift for you in this safe-deposit box."

"What do you mean, Manuel? I've barely gotten started. I need to find out more." You search his face, but you see nothing, no anger, no fear, no worry.

"It is time to go. Good-bye."

When you reach the airport, you open the box with the key. In it is a note. It says:

THE PLUMED SERPENT,
THE MOST POWERFUL GOD
OF THE MAYAS, WISHES YOU
LUCK. GO BACK WHERE YOU
CAME FROM AND STUDY YOUR
OWN COUNTRY. MAYBE YOU
CAN HELP YOUR PEOPLE.
THEY ARE IN DANGER.

In the box is a gold figure of a snake with feathers near its head. It is small, carved with great detail and the golden, carved scales gleam. Turning around, you see Tom who smiles and moves towards you.

The End

The left hand opens slowly, revealing a small clay figure. It is a good luck charm from Manuel to you.

You smile and Manuel smiles back. There is a puff of purple smoke and Manuel vanishes. You stare at the spot where he was standing just a second before. On the floor is a bright green feather, small and stiff. Where are you, though?

Your trip is over for now. Still no sign of Tom!

The End

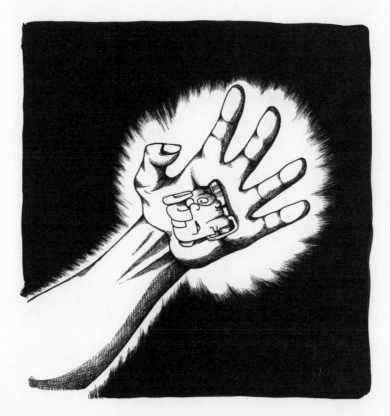

110

You give in to the Toltecs. After all, you couldn't find your way back to Chichen Itza if you tried. The trail back to Teotihuacan is long and hot. You and Xha and the twelve other prisoners are guarded by three Toltecs. Food is scarce and you are all hungry. Night is a welcome relief and sleep comes easily.

The route avoids settlements, and there seems to be no hope of escape. Finally, you arrive at the huge city, Teotihuacan, and the Temple of the Sun and the Moon. It is a magnificent city surrounded by mountains. The huge temple pyramids, connected by the Highway of the Dead, remind you of modern apartment towers.

You are thrown in with another group of prisoners and questioned by three Toltecs.

"Where did you come from? Who are you? What are you after?"

You answer as best you can, but they don't really believe or understand you. They offer you a choice by holding a fistful of straws. The bottom of each straw has been dipped in red, blue or yellow dye. You close your eyes and pick a straw.

If you draw a red straw, turn to page 131.

If you draw a blue straw, turn to page 122.

If you draw a yellow straw, turn to page 39.

What a bind you are in!

Guiding a Toltec raiding party going to Chichen Itza is dangerous. If you are captured by the Mayans, you will be accused of being a traitor. But your chances for escaping from the Toltecs seem better if you find Chichen Itza. If only you had some help!

Stepping over a tree trunk, you lift your leg high. Without even a rattle of warning, a large snake strikes. The fangs sink deep into your leg. The eyes of the beast glare at you. You begin to faint, but then the snake turns into a feathered bird! It is the Plumed Serpent—mystical god of the Mayas. In a deep tone of command the serpent tells you that he has chosen you as the new leader of the people.

With courage and pride you step forward. You seem a foot taller than before. Your eyes shine with power. The Toltecs fall down and tremble with fear.

If you accept this royal privilege, turn to page 21.

If you see this as an opportunity to escape the Toltecs, turn to page 13.

112

You decide to go it alone. It is a tight squeeze. You would get bruised and cut as you inch through the narrow opening in the sharp rocks without the protection of your wetsuit. At one point you think you are not going to make it.

Finally you are inside the cave. You remove the aqualung and head toward the treasure hoard.

IT'S GONE! Someone got there before you. You stand there empty handed, feeling foolish and disappointed.

Time waits for no one . . .

The End

You find a group of professional divers in Merida and lead them to the cave.

They place a small dynamite charge in the cave entrance. There is a muffled roar, the water foams and bubbles and grows murky with sand and mud. The cave mouth is open. The treasure is where you remembered it being. You start bringing up the gold.

Then a jeep arrives. Four uniformed Mexican officials get out.

"Congratulations! You have found the lost jewels of the Mayans. Our government will be very happy with your work." The man smiles. The other three start loading the gold and gems into their jeep.

You realize that you don't really mind after all. The Mayan treasure rightfully belongs to the people of Mexico, who are their descendants. You are glad that you were able to restore the treasure to its real owners. And you like being the center of attention. The government invites you to Mexico City and honors you at a dinner in the Mexican Natural History Museum where the jewels will be displayed.

The End

114

The road to Merida is narrow, dusty and bumpy. Every face on the bus seems to be staring at you. You wonder if they know that you are an agent of the police. You get a creepy feeling up and down your spine.

Once you are in Merida, you place a call to a man who runs a jewelry shop. His name is Julio. As the police suggested, he is the contact for the Red Hand gang. To your surprise, they are a fine group of people. They believe that they must fight so that the poor can have land to farm and a chance to make a good living. They tell you about the government that favors the rich and punishes the poor. They welcome you into their ranks.

Late one night as you sit around a table in the cellar of an old hotel, you feel that now is the time for a decision. Should you join them, tell them who you are, and become a triple agent, feeding the police the wrong information, or should you continue on as a spy in their midst? So far you have only heard talk, you have seen no proof of their dedication to the poor. Tom is nowhere to be seen.

If you believe them and decide to fight for their cause, turn to page 120.

If you don't believe them and decide to spy on them, turn to page 121.

Cancun is like a giant amusement park—crowded, noisy, filled with tourists. You don't know where to begin looking for Tom or for the Red Hand gang. Your only lead is the head bellman at the ritziest hotel on the strip.

That night you contact him. Big mistake! You vanish into the angry sea!

The End

116

The invitation to stay is a good idea. You are exhausted. You didn't bargain for storms at sea, or fights with priests, or raids on neighboring towns. Your head spins at the thought of the places you have been and the things you have done. You could use a rest after all that you have been through. The Arawak Indians are a peaceful people who gather fruit from the jungle and take fish from the sea, and that sounds about right to you.

A month passes. You are tanned by the sun. But now it is time to get back to the search for Tom. Isla Mujeres is a good lead, but now you hear rumors from a member of the crew that Tom, or someone like Tom, has been imprisoned in Chichen Itza and that the story about Isla Mujeres was to put you on the wrong scent.

If you return to Chichen Itza, turn to page 123.

If you go to Isla Mujeres, turn to page 126.

You stay on the island for a few days' rest. Once again the order comes to cast off, and your boat heads toward the coast of Yucatan. The sea is still rough, but the worst is over now. The night sky is clear, and the stars are your points for navigation. The captain and the crew know a great deal about the stars. The Mayans have learned about the constellations and the planets, especially Venus, which is both the evening and the morning star.

You pull into a small fishing village for new supplies, and then continue on up the coast, stopping at settlements, trading food stuffs and ornamental necklaces. Weeks pass, and the life is such a pleasant one, you decide never to return to modern times. You forget about bustling cities, deadlines, inflation, and pollution. This is the life for you. You hope that Tom has found a similar life.

But what happens when the potion wears off?

If you fight the potion wearing off,
turn to page 127.

If you let things take their course, turn to page 128.

You organize a medical team. But talk as you might, no one will join you to travel to any of the towns where there is sickness. You want to convince them to bury the dead, burn down the houses and huts, and cover the garbage with earth. Everyone thinks you are nuts.

"The gods are angry with us," they tell you. "There is nothing that we can do. It is said that we will all die. Maybe it is our time." You hear this over and over again.

"But we have to do something. We can't let all these people die." You plead with two priests.

"Go away. It is the will of the gods that these people will die. Leave us alone. The sickness hasn't come here yet, maybe we have pleased the gods."

Then two days later it happens. A woman takes sick and dies in one day. Then two men get the sickness. Children fall easy prey to the plague. Life in the once busy town comes to an end as the sickness sweeps through, actually wiping out the population.

Lucky for you the time potion prevents the plague from getting you. But it is time to leave. You call for Manuel to return you to the present.

The End

You depart Tulum. For days your boat travels up the coast, avoiding the small towns. The captain wants no chance of landing in a place where there is plague.

Finally you reach the coast close to Chichen Itza. You arrange to be taken through the jungle to the city. Once there, you beg the priests to take sanitary measures to prevent the spread of the plague. They regard you with dislike and fear. They won't hear of your suggestions about killing rats, burning garbage, tearing down old thatch-roofed buildings, or boiling the water. They warn you to leave or they will kill you for interfering with their beliefs.

"You are evil. You must not interfere with the normal way of the world," says the head priest. "The Lords of Xibila don't like your kind!"

If you obey the priests and leave quietly, turn to page 129.

If you ignore their threats, turn to page 130.

You started out in search of Tom, but now you are a member of the revolutionary Red Hand gang. You and your group do not use violence to reach your goals. You don't kidnap people; you don't hijack planes; you don't blow up buildings. Instead, you talk with the people. You encourage them to demand elections, to demand land reform. You teach them about Mexican law and how to use it. You give them hope and belief. But the work is dangerous. There are people who want to stop the Red Hand at any cost.

Your life is in constant danger. But you are committed to your work as a revolutionary.

The End

You have heard of revolutionaries before, and you don't believe this group is really interested in the people. You suspect they keep the money they collect at the meetings.

When you refuse to go on a mission chosen for you, they suddenly turn on you.

"You are a spy! You are our enemy."

They tie you up. The ropes bite into your wrists. Blood dampens the hemp. After two days, when your bones ache and your body wants to cry out for help, they come to you. "You are too dangerous to let go. We have held a meeting. We are sorry, but you must die."

To your amazement Tom appears with the leader.

"This one is no threat. I'll be responsible."

You are freed and Tom says, "Leave. And don't come back."

The End

Blue is a magic color. Only one of the straws was colored blue! You are now chosen to be a messenger to the Toltec god, Smoking Mirror.

Dressed in royal robes of blue and red, you are led to the top of the Pyramid of the Sun, tied to a small stone table and left to meet Smoking Mirror.

It's the end for you. You are to be sacrificed.

The End

You reluctantly leave your island paradise. It takes three tough weeks to get to Chichen Itza.

The marketplace is crowded with people dressed in brilliant reds, golds and blues. A great feast is in progress with chicken, iguana and bowls of maize, tomatoes and hot chilies. Mayans from all over have come to join in the ceremonies and rituals. People fill the enormous courtyards, chanting and singing.

Priests march about, followed by attendants. Warriors gather in groups, standing rigidly, looking fierce and stern.

The people are excited about a big sacrifice planned for later in the day.

Turn to page 124.

At the sound of a huge gong, the crowds fall silent. The priests march through the throngs to El Castillo—the great pyramid. They mount the steps. At the top of the steps the head priest raises his arms to the sun, and at that precise moment, the moon passes in front of the sun. Sudden darkness envelops the area. People are frightened. The priest drops his arms. When the sun once again shines as the moon continues its course, the people cheer. The ceremony has been a success. No sacrifice is needed.

You watch, amused by the way the priests have used knowledge of a solar eclipse to impress their people. Knowledge can be power.

As a token of good will, the victims prepared for sacrifice are released; one of them is Tom!

The End

126

You wait for a boat going to Isla Mujeres. Late one evening, you are sitting next to your fire near a small rocky hill. Thick brush surrounds you. Without warning, a band of warriors rush at you. Arrows fill the air. Your guide is killed. You fight back as best you can, knocking down two of your attackers with stones. Then you run. But an arrow hits you in the side. It's a poisoned arrow. Everything grows hazy, blurry, distant. The world seems to be spinning about your head. Your tongue feels thick and dry. There is darkness. You are finished.

The End

There must be some way to stay in the past! You just can't go back to the modern world!

The time potion wears off little by little. One day you look around and all of your new friends begin to fade slightly. They become less distinct each day, until finally there is no one around you. You are alone. You are sitting in the sand listening to the waves crash on the beach.

"Help, Help! I don't want to be here."

There is no one to hear you.

The End

What did you expect? You really can't hold onto the past. Time moves. You were given a glimpse into the past—but only a glimpse. You belong to the present and the future.

For you, your journey to the past has ended. The present and the future are before you.

The End

The priests are too powerful to challenge. They are in charge, and even the nobles and the best artists are frightened of them. It has not always been that way: Until recent time, the priests were respected, but the chief and his advisors were the actual rulers. Now, when the people are frightened by something like the plague, the priests and their predictions about the future become very important.

The people are frightened now. They move away from Chichen Itza in groups with a few belongings. Some head south to the jungles and the low-lying hills. Others go to the coast, and still others go west.

The feast days and ceremonies at the great pyramids and the games in the ball court draw fewer and fewer people. Fear has done its work better that the actual plague. The lifeblood of Chichen Itza drains away as the people leave searching for a better future.

The End

The noble who rules the area lives in a large palace, surrounded by servants. Six guards try to stop you. But the chief overhears your argument with the guards.

"Let this person come in," he says. "Well, what do you have to say?"

"I want to help. I know how we can stop this sickness."

You explain that the sickness can be stopped if rats are killed, water boiled, and the garbage buried. He listens intently and agrees to give it careful thought. These are new ideas, and he isn't sure that they will work.

But it is too late. The plague has spread, and soon Chichen Itza is filled with sickness.

You have witnessed one of the reasons for the decline of the Mayans. You are safe because you are only a time traveler and soon you will return to the present.

Dr. Lopez greets you in Merida saying, "The Mayans were great people, but all civilizations one day fall."

The End

Red leads to a job with the workers at the Pyramid of the Moon. You are shown how to chip and carve delicate patterns in stone that decorate the hallways and secret chambers of this magnificent pyramid. Heads of serpents, fierce faces with bulging eyes, and feathered birds are carved in stone.

All day you hammer and chip, following lines drawn on the stone by the Toltec priest-artists. Fine stone dust clogs your mouth and nose. Your eyes water constantly.

Then one day you are amazed to see six people in modern drip dry clothes walking toward you. One of them waves. Then they all wave. You run toward them but are stopped by an invisible wall of time.

You can't get back to the present time. Forever more, you must chip away at the stone carvings in the great Pyramid of the Moon.

The End

GLOSSARY

Cenote – *Cenotes* are deep water holes found throughout the Mayan region of the Yucatan. They are a by-product of the unique geology of the area. Ground water seeps down through the soft limestone becoming pure and colored green or blue in some cases. *Cenotes* provided the ancient Mayans with access to water during times of drought and were revered.

Chichen Itza – An ancient city in Mexico that was part of the Mayan Civilization. Chichen Itza is located in the central part of the Yucatan. It is a popular tourist destination because of its well-preserved ruins. Chichen Itza has steep steps and looks like a pyramid without the pointy top.

Isla Mujeres – A small island near Cancun, off the southeast coast of Mexico. It got its name from the Spanish word "mujeres", meaning women.

Maize – A type of indigenous (local) corn that is yellow in color and high in starches and sugars. Maize has been grown in Mexico and Central and South America for thousands of years. It is the "parent" of modern corn. Even today, maize is a major crop and used throughout the region to make everyday foods like tortillas and cereal.

Mayan – A Mayan is a member of an ancient and advanced civilization that existed in the Yucatan (what is now Mexico), Belize and Guatemala. These Indian groups shared similar languages and physical features. The Mayan civilization was strong between 300 and 900 AD. It was known for its design of buildings, pottery and making an accurate calendar through the use of astronomy. People of Mayan descent still consider themselves Mayan even if they now live in Mexico.

Nunnery – The Nunnery is a building at the ancient Mayan temple complex at Uxmal. It was named by Spanish conquistadores after nunneries in Europe, buildings where nuns would live. Today archeologists and anthropologists believe the Nunnery was used by the ancient Mayans as a school for shamans and healers.

Potion – A mix of liquids that can be medicine, liquor or poison. Potions are sometimes referred to as having "magical" qualities.

Rain forest – A dense, tropical forest that gets at least 100 inches (254 centimeters) of rain each year. Sometimes called Tropical Rain Forests, these areas are known for their lush greenery and many species of plants, animals, birds and insects.

Safe-deposit Box – A fireproof storage container, usually a locked box, where valuables are kept safe. Safe-deposit boxes are often found in bank vaults. If you want to protect valuables like gems or important documents for a long time, a safe-deposit box is a good idea.

Spanish Conquistadors – Conquerors who came from Spain. They sailed to Mexico and Peru in the 16th Century. Their mission was to defeat the Indian civilizations and claim land for Spain.

UFO – An acronym for Unidentified Flying Object. UFOs are sometimes called flying saucers. No one knows where they come from or if they are real. UFOs are considered to have their beginnings beyond Earth.

Underworld – A word from ancient Greek and Roman Mythology that means the world of the dead. The underworld is also referred to as Hades or Hell. In ancient times, it was believed that when a bad person died their spirit would go to the underworld.

Uxmal – An old city in southeastern Mexico that has well preserved ruins including the Temple of the Magicians. The Temple of the Magicians, at 100 feet, is the tallest structure in Uxmal. Legend has it that a magician-god called Itzamna built the pyramid in one night all by himself.

CREDITS

Character/Art Designer: Vorrarit Pornkerd. Vorrarit was born in February 1982 in Bangkok, Thailand. He graduated from Faculty of Decorative Arts, Silpakorn University, where he majored in Visual Communication Design (Illustration). After graduation, he worked as a Designer for Digicrafts Co. Ltd. He is currently a Character Designer and illustrator for Tajkanit Partnership.

Illustrator: Sasiprapa Yaweera. Sasiprapa was born in October 1981 in Suphanburi, a province of Thailand. She studied at Suphanburi College of Fine Arts and continued to pursue her love for the arts in Bunditpatanasilpa Institute, from which she has just graduated. Today she is a promising young illustrator with Tajkanit Partnership.

Cover Artist: Jintanan Donploypetch. Jintanan was born in September 1981 in Nakorn Pathom, Thailand and has just graduated from Faculty of Decorative Arts, Silpakorn University. During her studies, she collected numerous awards including "Best Animation" from the Thailand Animation Association. She has worked as an Art Designer at Kantana Animation House and is now an Artist at Tajkanit Partnership.

This book was brought to life by a great group of people:
   Shannon Gilligan, Publisher
   Gordon Troy, General Counsel
   Jason Gellar, Sales Director
   Melissa Bounty, Senior Editor
   Stacey Boyd, Designer

   Thanks to everyone involved!

Buy the paperback version of this title and others at www.cyoa.com.

ABOUT THE AUTHOR

R. A. MONTGOMERY has hiked in the Himalayas, climbed mountains in Europe, scuba-dived in Central America, and worked in Africa. He lives in France in the winter, travels frequently to Asia, and calls Vermont home. Montgomery graduated from Williams College and attended graduate school at Yale University and NYU. His interests include macro-economics, geo-politics, mythology, history, mystery novels, and music. He has two grown sons, a daughter-in-law, and two granddaughters. His wife, Shannon Gilligan, is an author and noted interactive game designer. Montgomery feels that the new generation of people under 15 is the most important asset in our world.

**For games, activities and other fun stuff,
or to write to R. A. Montgomery,
visit us online at CYOA.com**